DISPOSABLES

PRASAD DESHPANDE

Made with ♥ on the Notion Press Platform
www.notionpress.com

Contents

Preface

As the time passes, the mentality of humans is getting more and more, sick...

For want of money, property, name and fame – people tend to use others as stepping stones only to forget about them once they are on the next planned level. Gone are the days where a word given by anyone remained solemn even if it meant death.

This is a fictional story about such incidences, sure to keep you wondering whenever the twists in this story unfold.

As usual, the statutory warning...

This work is entirely fiction and any resemblance to anyone, any place or any incidence is purely coincidental – or – maybe, your wild imagination... J

People appear to you the way they want you to see them and when the "real they" appear – you are left flabbergasted looking at their reality. You simply do not understand as to how you should react...

Without wasting any more time – let us start with the story.

CHAPTER ONE

He looked out of the window into the darkness. The train was now at its best speed. Odd shaped sizes loomed up in quick succession, reflected by the dim lights of the compartment.

He was unmoved by the buzz inside the crowded compartment. He had a fixed fiery stare at the darkness outside.

He looked at the watch. According to his calculation, the train should be passing over a bridge on a wide river, crossing its vast expanse.

Any moment now ... He pulled out his mobile phone and thought for a moment. He looked at the calling card that got pulled out along with his phone. It showed "V K Motors".

Unwittingly, he crumpled the card even as he clenched his fist. Sure enough, the train did start passing over a bridge over the vast expanse of a river.

He smiled with a triumphant anticipation and threw the crumpled card along with his phone into the flowing river as the train passed over it.

He then, had a glum look on his face even as the feelings of remorse rebelled within – he realized – he had murdered about a dozen good men or more in his frenzy and in the heat of emotions ... all for nothing...

What difference was it going to make if he now commits another murder – *this time in cold blood...*

CHAPTER TWO

His thoughts wandered into the past. Not six months ago – he was living a simple and peaceful life.

He owned a motor repair shop in a smallish town. He had worked hard to see it prosper and his repair shop was now famous in that town.

He had upgraded his skills and the equipment to cater to high cost cars. Almost every rich man in that town trusted him with his expensive cars.

Every year, toward the start of monsoon, he used to take a month long vacation. His repair centre remained closed with all helping hands off with a paid holiday.

He used to visit his near and dear relatives during this time to keep the bonds of relations alive.

This year, he had decided to extend the vacation to two months. His cousin at a distant smallish town wanted to set up a motor repair workshop and wanted him to help him set it up.

He was meticulous and he informed all his regular customers about the temporary closure of his workshop and then accordingly had boarded the south bound train. The overnight journey took him to his cousin.

He was happy at the warm welcome by his family and he didn't waste any time. He started working right away and started to train his cousin.

Soon ... The business started to grow and the customers started to pour in. Then, one of the esteemed businessmen in that town entrusted them with one of his expensive cars.

He worked wonders on that car. The owner was immensely pleased and promised him that his entire fleet would be entrusted to them.

The next day, the businessman returned with another car.

While he was inspecting the car a bike crashed on to it causing ugly dent. He demanded that the guys on the bike pay for the damage they had done and the conversation took an ugly turn. The guys were tough guys and in the heat of the argument, he lost control on his temper and thrashed them senseless.

The police had taken his custody for the fight and put him in remand. The business person was made aware of what had happened and used his clout to get him released. The rich guy knew that whatever happened was to get the damage charges out of those tough guys for the dent they had caused.

He worked on that car giving it the finest polished look much to the joy of the businessman. Soon ... other businessmen from the town started to entrust their cars to that repair workshop.

He realized that they were interconnected with many interlinked businesses. The cousin's repair workshop started to flourish and he was happy for his cousin.

CHAPTER THREE

About a couple of days later he realized that the expensive cars of these businessmen were brought in and driven away by a girl in her early twenties.

She used to drop one car and pick the finished one, pay for the bill of repair and zoom away.

All his life – he had been alone and had buried himself deep in his work. He not only loved his work but was passionate and possessive about it.

He never had the time, nor had he bothered to look around at any female or even his regular female customers, however, he found himself attracted to this smiling young woman who drove the expensive cars of all these businessmen.

She had something different in her attitude. She knew he was getting attracted to her and didn't mind it. She always wore expensive branded garments. Her looks were attractive and neat – head to toe.

Her smile and her soft voice seemed too attractive. To him, she resembled a combination of few famous female stars. Without any real intention of any commitment, he started to slowly drift toward her.

These feelings were new to him.

Over the next few weeks, their conversation grew. She seemed interested in him and his work and kept asking questions to know him better. He was glad about her interest in him and kept talking.

Everyday his heart longed to see her drive in with a car. He used to be restless whenever she failed to turn up.

One day he had a sudden realization – the workshop she used to visit belonged to his cousin. Why – he didn't even belong to that town. His own business was a flourishing one and was miles away from this town.

She seemed rich with rich expensive tastes and wasn't a correct match for him. With huge and difficult internal conflict – he started to control the feelings he felt for her.

He started concentrating more and more on the workshop than sitting on the counter. He knew he had to return and used most of his time to train his cousin and his aides.

Soon – it was time for him to return to his town. The vacation was over. He had to be back to his town – his workshop and his customers – and his life.

He did hope to see her one more time – just to bid a goodbye – before he returned to his town. The day of departure passed off and she didn't visit the workshop. He was ready to go... Again, it was the overnight train.

The season of monsoon had now set in firm and it was raining heavy. He said bye to his cousin and his family and boarded the pre-booked cab to the railway station.

CHAPTER FOUR

The visibility was poor as the heavy rain lashed the windscreen of the cab. They stopped for a moment even as he shifted to the front seat next to the driver to guide him, the road. Two people were better equipped to watch the road better.

They had to take a longer route. Many roads were facing a water logging problem making it impossible to pass through them.

They were passing through a narrow uphill lane on the edge of a short cliff by the raging sea when he saw a female figure loom up ahead. She was struggling with a trolley suitcase and a huge handbag – trying to pull it up the slope.

He waived to the driver to pull up beside her, pulled down the window and looked outside...

"Hey – you need any help?"

"Yes. I do. I am trying to get to the railway station for the night train. I am unable to get any transportation here. If you could, please, help me reach any place where I can get a transport."

"I am on my way to the railway station. You can ride this cab. We will drop you off."

With some difficulty, she managed to push her bags onto the back seat and thankfully took a seat beside them. They had a silent ride till they reached the railway station.

The cab was already paid for and he jumped out in haste and got his baggage from the boot and helped the lady with her baggage.

"Thank you." She said smiling and then looked at him in astonishment. He had the same look on him. She was the girl who drove those expensive cars.

"You?" They both uttered at the same time. After an awkward pause, he told her that he was returning to his town as his business was situated there. He casually asked her as to where she was intending to travel – his heart hoping that she would travel in the same direction. This way, he would be able to spend some time in her – a girl who had brought these emotions of longing into him. She sneezed as an answer to his question. He realized that she was completely drenched in the heavy rain and needed to dry up.

"The railway rest room is over there." He gently suggested her, "Let's go there – you can dry yourself and put on some warm clothes – else you may fall sick."

She nodded a meek approval at his suggestion and they made their way toward the restroom. He patiently awaited her return, keeping a careful watch over her trolley bag. She emerged out of the restroom wearing a traditional Punjabi suit with her dupatta wound around her head & partially covering her face to keep herself warm.

"My train will be leaving in about 30 minutes – I guess – I will have to buy any ticket that is left out – what about you?"

To his dismay she burst into tears and started to weep. He didn't know what to say or react. He kept looking at her in dismay. In a moment or so she controlled her emotions.

"I'm leaving this town. I haven't planned anything yet. I don't know what I will be doing or where I should go..."

"Does your family know that you are leaving?" he asked a bit concerned.

"I don't have a family. I am alone in this world."

"Oh! Sorry I asked."

"I understand. Please don't feel sorry about it – it's not your fault. If you don't mind, is it okay if I travel with you to your town? Maybe, by that time I may get enough time to decide what I want to do."

His heart jumped within – this was something he had wished and his wish seemed to be coming true.

"Of course – you can..." he said in a delighted tone, "Let's go and buy our tickets."

They quickly made their way to the ticket counter for the last minute booking. The train was a special train and only those who had valid tickets were allowed to board it.

The train was heavily booked and they were fortunate enough to get the last two tickets left – they were for a first class coupe – very expensive.

"Vicky Kundan" he affirmed his name to the booking person at the counter and looked at her realizing that he didn't even know her name.

"Rekha, Rekha Meerut" she informed him smiling at his generosity and her blessed luck.

They made their way to the coupe they had booked and boarded the train minutes before the train rumbled out of the station into the pouring darkness.

He stood in the corridor even as she shut the door of the coupe to change into softer, comfortable and warmer clothes.

CHAPTER FIVE

He was feeling cold. He had had no chance to change into dry ones since the time he met her on that desolate road.

He rushed into the coupe as soon as she opened the door, picked up dry clothes and rushed to the washroom toward the end of the bogie.

He returned to find that she had managed to put up a make shift drying line for the wet clothes inside the coupe. Her wet clothes already hung there. She took his wet clothes he held in his hand and put them up on the drying line.

This was all new for him. He had stayed alone the major part of his life and was not accustomed to someone else doing these simple daily chores.

The ticket checker entered with another railway staff member who presented them with complimentary meals that came along with the expensive fare of their journey.

They devoured the meal with appetite after the checker left and he carried the disposable food packages to the bin next to the bathroom in the bogie and settled down in the coupe.

She was looking out of the window – lost in some deep thought – a tear rolled down her cheek...

"I'm sorry to ask – I know it's none of my business. However, I feel that you should talk and let out the feelings that are troubling you. That will make you feel better..." he gently tried to strike a conversation with her.

"What will you do? I don't want to bother a good man like you with my woes."

"I don't know yet. However, I know – I can at least give you a patient ear. Perhaps, I might be able to suggest something that could help you..."

She looked at him with moist eyes. He could see her struggle to get her words out.

"It's okay if you don't want to speak about it ... anyways ... we do have to part our ways when we reach our destination in the morning."

"You are a good man – you really are..." she said, now looking directly into his eyes, "maybe, you are right. Speaking my troubles out could ease off my pain."

He sat upright – all his attention to hear her out.

"Don't know how and where to begin. I belong to a distant town – Dehradoon. I did my schooling at CJM and graduated from Doon Business School."

He looked at her in awe. She was educated and he was a college dropout.

"My father passed away when I was young and studying school. My uncle sponsored my education till graduation. My mother was a lady full of self-respect. She didn't want my uncle's favour of him sponsoring my education and providing us money to look after ourselves. So she moved over to his town and took up a job in his fields and his office to pay off for the expenses – whatever she could."

He looked at her, his expression blank, wanting her to continue.

She smiled at him and continued, "It was during my college days that I realized how bad this world is. Knowing that I am alone and I stay at the hostel sponsored by my uncle and that I spend whatever I have cautiously – rich kids – wolves to be precise – started hounding me – always showing their readiness to spend money for anything I need – no matter what the cost – just to take advantage of me. When I politely refused, they started threatening me with dire consequences. I somehow managed to keep them away from me and stay safe till I graduated."

"Go on..." he prodded.

"My uncle already had borne the expense of my education and hostel. Being my mother's daughter, I didn't want to burden him further. My mother always had insisted on self-reliance. So I started to apply for jobs even as I neared the final semester."

"Seems like a good choice." he said.

"Soon the fate smiled and I got a job – location was New Delhi. It was for a back office which involved a lot of data processing. I proved to my boss that I was the best. I thought he understood my problems. I used to stay in not so good and a kind of bit dangerous suburbs. I used to travel at least 2 hours – one way to reach office and similar time to return. My boss arranged my stay in a flat at a good locality nearby to our office. I was so happy because now this arrangement gave me more time so that I could pursue further studies as well saved me money. This also meant that with further studies, I would be able to get a better and a higher paying job and that way I can return the money to my uncle who had spent it on my education."

He was lost in her big, innocent eyes that kept looking at him and his interest.

"I was wrong. My boss allowed me to the luxurious flat and the good locality so that I get accustomed to that lifestyle... one day ... he told me that I no longer would be able to occupy the flat and use those facilities. He saw my dejection. I had left my suburban flat and had not anticipated this move. He asked me to vacate the flat he had offered within a month."

She held back the tears that were ready to flow again.

"I didn't know what to do. That day he had given me extra workload to be completed and had offered to drive me to my accommodation. When we drove back – he subtly hinted that he would be able to allow me to stay on in that flat – provided I accepted to compromise and yield to his wolfish demands – he also promised to me that he would double my salary & perks. All I needed to do was allow him to enjoy my body."

"What the ..." he choked in his anger.

"I told him that I needed time to consider this and may take a couple of months to make up my mind for the compromise because this was a tough decision. He agreed. That moment, I had decided that I will leave his job and search some other one. But, the company I worked for was a well-known service provider in the country and almost every other company person knew him. In the process I also realized that there were wolves in every damn office I visited for an interview. He using his clout made sure that I do not get any other job..."

She heaved a sigh as she continued, "Fortunately – I had a friend in the town we met. She was getting married and was settling abroad. She helped me get into her job and her position. Knowing what I was facing and knowing that my boss could mess up even in this town ... she helped me forge my documents and identity and I took this false identity called Rekha Meerut and started working here. I was able to start my life – anew."

"Wow!" he could only manage to mutter this word.

She looked at him with sad eyes as she spoke in continuation.

"It was all good and I enjoyed my job as a personal assistant. My boss here headed a consortium of various businesses. There were about 15 directors in that consortium. Looking at my work efficiency – they all wanted me to assist them as well. My boss and I agreed – and my salary grew manifold. Being their personal assistant, I used to attend their business meets, collate their data, keep the inputs they needed ready. But ... alas ..."

CHAPTER SIX

"So – then what happened?" he gently eased her into saying it all.

"I realized – it's difficult to live alone in this world."

"I understand." He said, "Even I am alone in this world. I have few relatives spread around the country. No parents, no siblings."

"You are a man and a strong one."

"What do you mean?"

"You didn't see me when I saw you for the first time. That was when you were thrashing those bid bad bikers."

"Oh! Did you? – Well I'm sorry for that display of rage."

"You don't have to be sorry for that, they deserved that thrashing. When police took you into their custody – I told my boss that you were in trouble because you tried to help us and it was his responsibility to help you out of this situation."

"I should thank you for this favour." he said with gratitude, "If your boss was so good – why are you leaving such a well settled life – so abrupt?"

"It's difficult to be alone in this world – in fact – it's a crime to be all alone in this big bad world – especially – if you are a girl and a good looking one."

"I don't understand." he said in a bid to carry on with the conversation, he now was realizing that she indeed looked fabulous and had a perfectly sexy body.

"You're a man and a strong one. You got enough strength to thrash anyone who dares behave any kind of nonsense with you. I'm a girl. I don't have physical strength like you. Every night – I do get a terrible sleep – not knowing when some wolf might try to molest me or take advantage of me being alone."

"You are good looking and well educated. Why don't you find someone suitable, get married and do away with all this lonely life? – you also will get good protection from your husband – whoever he may be and never have to sleep a terrible sleep."

"I have been hounded by these wolves called men – right from the age when I started to grow up. I haven't met any man as of yet who is above these animal feelings. Today, my boss called me to his farmhouse with few important papers. It was close to my accommodation. I reached there even as clouds started to gather. While I awaited his next instruction, I overheard them discuss that today was the right opportunity to exploit and maul me..."

She started to weep again – much to his dismay.

"I somehow managed to make a run – away from there to my accommodation. On the way – I decided to leave everything in the town including my job and leave for good. It was raining heavily by the time I started and wasn't able to find any transport to the station. You came along and helped me – you are helping me even as of now."

"Oh! That's nothing to mention about..." he waived a hand in pleasure of being in good terms with her.

"I was scared when your cab stopped by my side – but, then I saw you and knew I was safe."

"What if, I had turned an animal and hounded you?"

"No – you couldn't – at least give me that credit. I have met so many men that I know the difference between a wolf, a sheep and a man – you are a man alright. I know that at one point of time – you were infatuated by me during my visits to the workshop. A wolf would have hounded me for persuasion, a sheep would have remained in naive, gutless infatuation – you are a man – you conquered the rising infatuation within you and remained professional. You started treating me as professionally as you did your other customers – I wish – I could marry a man like you..."

He was taken aback by this bold statement.

"I know – you think that this wouldn't be possible looking at our differences – believe me – a girl always wants to marry a man – his work, education doesn't mean anything relevant to her." he was too stunned to react and she realized this, "I understand – this was out of blue. To me – meeting a man like you was a boon in itself. I'm sick of fighting all my battles alone. I know it would be ages before I meet any other real man like you. The sheep and the wolves are everywhere – but a man like you is rare. I have to try."

He looked at her blank. His mind was blank. He could say nothing.

"I guess – I'll shut up and let you think." she said and opened the door of the coupe and stood in the passage way watching the darkness outside.

He didn't know what to say or what his decision should be. She definitely was a girl of dreams for anyone. He was happy that she considered him suitable enough to get married to him.

He looked at her – she was standing, resting her shoulder to the wall of the train looking out of the window. She had let loose her well maintained hair and her body looked too attractive to him.

He also realized that they had a difference about the way they lived their lives. She was much more educated than him. She had rich, exquisite and expensive tastes of living. On other hand, he had led his life a simple and humble way. There was no match. He finally decided to tell her about every difference between them and let her decide which he knew she would finally reject the idea of marrying him.

He looked at her – she now stood resting her back to the wall – looking intently at him. She knew that he now was ready to talk to her and entered the coupe closing the door behind her. She sat opposite him, looking at him with wide dreamy anticipation...

CHAPTER SEVEN

He told her about his simple living and modest earnings. He also cautioned her about the difference between their living standards and styles.

He thought that listening to his honest confession about his simple living standards will make her rethink about her own proposal to get married to him.

She smiled wide at him, "Apart from being a man – you are True and Honest. You are the rarest species I can ever dream of meeting." she jumped out of her seat and knelt in front of him, "Please accept me as your wife. These expensive things mean nothing to me. I swear I will love wearing simple, cheap clothes you may buy. I will be happy to cook your meals, I will make your bed, will wash your clothes. I can use my education and experience to help you grow your business while keeping the counter for you while you work wonders on those expensive cars..."

"Well..." he could hardly speak as he looked at her kneeling in front of him – his heart was filled with pity for her and the pains she had been enduring – her struggle to lead a good, steady life. He looked at her again – this time, through eyes of a prospective groom & his heart approved her at once.

He smiled, "Yes – I will be the happiest man to have you as my wife."

His heart melted completely when he saw her blush.

"We will marry at the first opportunity once I speak to our priest."

"Now that you have agreed to marry me – Why wait?" she said even as he looked at her in disbelief, "Don't misunderstand me." She added hastily, "Do you believe in GOD?"

"Yes. I do."

"So do I." she smiled at him, she looked at her wrist watch, "In about 15 minutes, our train will pull into a station where it has a long halt. I have every reason to believe that our bogie will get stationed exactly in front of a huge and a beautiful temple which we should be able to see from here. I have seen it couple of times on my journey to visit my mother. We can pray and let GOD be the witness to our wedding. No better witness than HIM – right?"

He looked at her – a bit bewildered.

"Please do not take all I say in wrong way. Once I know, I am married to a wonderful man like you ... I will be able to experience the most peaceful & safe sleep. I have only been able to dream of such a sleep..."

"Do you believe in GOD who resides in a temple?"

She laughed playfully at this question & his confusion, "Didn't I tell you that I had to forge my true identity to escape any trace back to my ex-boss in Delhi? – My real name is RIYA ... I do believe in the GOD who resides in temples – I regularly do visit any temple around the vicinity where I stay..."

"If you now reveal your true identity now – will not your ex-boss at Delhi come tracking you down?"

"Once I'm married to you – I don't have to be scared of him or anyone else. You are there to protect me. Further – I will be helping you grow your business – not looking for a job where he can hamper my career progress – my career is now – You, your home, our life and our children – we, together, will create a beautiful life for ourselves..."

He looked at her relaxed smile and thought for a moment – not a bad idea – who else can be the best witness other than GOD... And with GOD as witness – the wedding does hold its values.

"Okay..." he said in agreement even as the train started to slow down in its approach into that station for its halt. He looked out of the window – sure enough, there was this huge, beautifully carved out temple bang opposite the window of their coupe...

"Let's pray and seek HIS blessings." she said and folded her hands and looked solemnly at the temple. He followed her action and folded his hands in a prayer.

"I, Riya, with all my heart & mind, accept Vicky Kundan as my wedded husband. O! GOD! – Please bless us and our married life together..." she said in a solemn voice and looked at him – he followed her suit and accepted her as his wife – his heart jumping and a mind full of joy. They prayed for few more minutes and looked at each other as they felt a small jolt of the train that had now started to move, ready to pick up motion toward her new home in the new town and a blessed married life.

She put her arms around him and held him tight hiding her face in his chest. With thumping heart, his fingers caressed the tresses of her long, soft, shiny hair.

She looked at him with moist eyes showing her relief from all her troubles and with a hope of a new, happy life ahead. She slowly put her lips upon his as they softly kissed.

"I got to tell you something important for both of us..." she said moving a bit away from him, "in our family, we don't indulge in sex for one year from the wedding unless – the girl gets desperate for it – after that – it's regular married life."

"Is that all?" he asked smiling.

"Yes – that's all. It's just for one year – no sex – but we can – hug and kiss each other as many times as we want."

"Done" he said in a promising tone and she hugged him again following with more intimate kisses.

CHAPTER EIGHT

The train reached his town in time. It was early in the morning and the town was yet to start its day.

He opened the main door to his motor repair centre & welcomed her inside. He then led her to a small flight of steps toward the back of the centre. They led to a couple of small bedrooms cum restrooms, adjacent to them was a small, shabby make shift kitchen type setup.

"This is where and how I live... You still have a chance to walk out – your way – Nobody, except GOD, knows how we married each other.

She looked around in confusion and a bit of a shock. The rooms were shabby indeed and definitely not up to her living standards.

"Which one's gonna be my room?" she asked.

He pointed out the first room next to the shabby kitchen, "That's going to be our bedroom."

"Oh! No! – Not for first year – I hope you remember your promise." she smiled and said "Okay – I take this room and you take the one next to the steps." saying thus, she entered the room, "Ugh! It's so dirty..."

"It's rarely been used and the whole place was shut for about 45 days and I never knew that I would return with a beautiful bride. I had no chance of cleaning or sprucing anything up... I do have a couple of days before I formally open the workshop for customers – I will get the cleaning done."

"We will get the cleaning done." she corrected him with a smile, "Could you get something for our breakfast in the meantime? – I have to think as to where to start the cleaning work..."

He smiled his approval and obediently left to fetch their breakfast. He returned with a pile of packed food packages.

"Hey! What's this?" she said looking at the pile.

"Breakfast as well our lunch... I don't want you to exert yourself the day you arrive in my life." he said and looked around at the cleaning and the changes in the arrangement she had done, "my word ... this place has a pleasantly changed looks ... now I understand why they say that it's a woman who makes or breaks the house..."

"You like it?"

"It's looking – Wow..."

"This is going to be my room, and that is going to be yours. I have also cleaned up kitchen so that I can cook our meals. I'll now take a bath and then we will have our breakfast."

For a few days, she kept in the interiors, cooking meals and washing clothes till he got a washing machine to help her. This reduced her work and she had much time left over. She decided to help him by sitting on the counter while he worked upon the expensive cars.

For the first few days, he was overwhelmed by the compliments which came from his regular customers. They were quite impressed by her presence at the counter. She was sweet, innocent and beautiful. This added the charm to the place. Those who were not his regular customers also showed interest in becoming his regular ones. His business grew.

About a month had passed and they were doing pretty good. While she managed kitchen and the counter, he was able to concentrate on the car repairs. Evening, they used to go out and he showed her around the town.

One day, about a month or so had passed she snuggled close to him and kissed him warm and soft.

"I want to start a business..."

"What?"

"I said, I want to start a business. That will add on the income."

"Why? Are my efforts less?"

"No honey ... But, I want to utilize my skills and my knowledge – so that I can earn as well and our efforts together can get a better education for our children to come ... Please understand."

"What sort of business are you planning?"

"You know Mrs Choksy? She is one of your customers who gets that Audi for maintenance ... she suggested me a business. Its ladies perfumes, beauty products and accessories. There is a huge market and only one or two ladies doing it. It's a fabulous opportunity..." she waited for his reaction.

"Do you think you can do it?"

"I am confident I can do it. Plus, Mrs Choksy will be there to guide me grow that business. Why not take a chance?"

"I am still not convinced, but if you feel confident, go ahead with it."

She snuggled still closer and kissed him, "There is a small catch... We need to invest first." she said a bit slowly.

"How much do you need to invest?"

"About Rupees two and a half lakh"

His heart sank "What!! I don't have that kind or free cash, nor do I earn that much."

"I don't know anyone in this town who can help me. See, if you can get someone to lend it. As per her calculation, this amount can be recovered in three months – and if you are good enough, two months. It's a low time period. See if anyone you know can help us." she kissed him again

CHAPTER NINE

He slept uncomfortable sleep. He couldn't afford the amount and he couldn't break her heart. This was the first time she had asked a favour out of him. And he knew he couldn't say no to her. He decided to ask his bank for loan and see how much he could manage.

He proceeded to the bank in the morning and waited for the bank manager to attend his application. To his surprise, the manager instantly approved his application. He said that he also sends his car to him for repair and maintenance and knew how honest and hard-working he was as a person.

He was happy to know that he was considered to be an asset and his overall bank standing was good. He also was happy because he had not failed Riya as a husband. He was able to support her need to stand on her own feet.

He happily entered his house. He deliberately looked frustrated.

"What happened?" Riya asked with anticipation.

"Well – I have to tell you something. You know I am a car mechanic. The bank manager knows that. His car is serviced by me. He knows me and my ability very well..."

"Did he sanction the loan?" She asked in an anxious tone.

"That's what I am about to tell you ..."

"Tell me na ..." she couldn't bear the suspense.

"Well – The bank manager looked at me and decided..."

"Tell na..." now her anxiety was almost to its peak.

"That I am eligible for the loan amount. He sanctioned the loan and here is the cash. Happy?"

She put her arms around him and kissed him away showing her happiness. All that she had planned would now be a reality and soon the gates of fortune would open for her. She was happy and her happiness flowed in her kisses to him.

She left the home after her kitchen chores and put on her best dress to meet Mrs Choksy. The venue to meet was the lounge at Grand club house. It was a well to do social club and resto-bar with a 24hr coffee house. It was also a 4 star accommodation with few halls for conference purpose.

She hired an auto and reached the place. She was a bit uncomfortable with low confidence as she entered the premise. She knew her best dress was a misfit and under graded in such a posh premise. She studied the ladies who walked in and out of the place and felt more uncomfortable. Not that, she had never visited such a place before, she didn't have an attire to visit this one.

As she looked around, her sight fell on Mrs Choksy who was sitting there and observing her with interest and studying her behaviour of less comfort and low confidence. She beckoned her to occupy the seat next to her and she gladly took the seat. She was more comfortable with Mrs Choksy beside her.

"You seem to be low on confidence." Mrs Choksy remarked.

"No. I'm just observing the crowd here and thinking how to approach. What I need to wear and how to carry myself in this crowd."

"Good. So you are ready to start I believe."

"Yes – if the money is good – I am ready."

"Don't worry dear, the town is full of rich people with rich wives who like beauty products and costly perfumes. You got the personality – only your clothes have to be more up to date. And your linguistic skills have to be perfect. Then nobody can stop you to earn that money. Soon, you will be driving an Audi of your own..."

Riya was pleased with this comment. She was attentive when Mrs Choksy explained the products and her mind was in over drive thinking about how she would go about getting her clients.

"Now – let me tell you about your clients. I don't deal with any of them they have egoistic problems with me because I am wife of their competitor. That is your chance."

"If I approach them and I sell these to them, how would you benefit?"

"Simple, you are joining under me with my reference. When you sell something, you get your commission and I get my royalty. That sets the records straight, I will indirectly earn from what you sell. When you are settled in this business, you can get someone like you under you and we both will earn royalties from whatever she sells. No work to be done – only enjoy the earnings."

"Wow! That seems to be good... I am all in to start. Let me know my clients."

"Now pay attention, one of them is arriving now. She is Mrs Kak. She stays here for 3 months and then goes to Chandigarh where she belongs, for another 3 months. When she goes there, she carries lots of items as gifts for her relatives. I believe she has a huge joint family. Beware of Mr Kak. He is a womaniser, especially when she is not in town. They have permanently booked a suit in this premise. They don't own any house here."

"Ok. Noted..."

"With her is Mrs Gupta. She is another of the rich bitches and spends lot of money to buy gifts to impress her friends and relatives. Mr Gupta is the largest dealer in iron and steel here and has all industries buying from him."

"Ok."

She kept on giving relevant information about more rich ladies and Riya kept noting that mentally. She was now confident in what she was going to do and how she was going to do it. She smiled at the prospect of all the money she would earn.

Once all the paperwork was done and required amount paid, she was ready to leave. She would collect the products from the store in the evening when all relevant paperwork from the company's end would be processed.

Leaving that premise, she proceeded to the cloth market where she spent money on clothes that would help her in her endeavour. She moved on to the accessory market and got the accessories that would enhance her style.

She was confident now that she had the basic requirement all bought and with her. She picked up the products and samples from the store and smiled – she knew what she had to do.

She hired and auto and all the way to her home, she was into planning what she had sought out to seek – mentally. Her plan was ready and she felt relaxed and determined.

CHAPTER TEN

Next day, she was ready in her new attire. He just kept looking at her beauty and glamour. She was devastatingly attractive. He wanted to take her in his arms but decided not to disturb her dress.

"How am I looking?" she asked him knowing he was totally stumped by her beauty.

"You are gorgeous, beautiful, attractive, sexy, mind boggling ..." he couldn't find enough words to describe her and she was happy about her looks ... she presented him a short sweet kiss not allowing him to touch her and left for her 1st day in business.

She reached Grand Club and entered it with confidence. She knew she had the right kind of dress and accessories that fit in the environment. She ordered for coffee and patiently waited for any client to arrive and then she would put on her action.

She looked around and saw Mr and Mrs Kak in a conversation with someone. Mr Kak looked around casually and his sight got arrested to the new glamour doll sitting in the lounge – Riya. She gave him a sweet smile and pointed towards his wife. He had a small conversation with his wife who got up and walked gracefully to Riya. His wife was beautiful too...

Riya got up as Mrs Kak approached her and smiled at her.

"Hi – I'm Riya – new to this town. You look beautiful."

Mrs Kak with praise form such a lovey girl smiled back at her, "Hi – I'm Mrs Kak, Wife of one of the richest businessman here. What brings you to this small town – you look like you have come here from a big city."

"Marriage – that's what brought me here and I have started a small business to be a big, rich business woman. The business is about rich perfumes and accessories and I'm soon planning to grow it into a fashion house. Just need time and attention of people like you who have an eye for delicate rich things."

Pleased with her flattery Mrs Kak was now interested in what sort of perfumes and accessories she had and asked her to show if she had any samples... Riya was intelligent enough to see what attracted Mrs Kak and pulled out some accessories right from ear-rings to bangles to anklets...

"Wow! – This stuff seems to be good. Some of it is pure gold."

"It's 18 carat gold plated – so it looks fabulous and actually nobody can tell it is gold plated – they all think it is real gold – for a one time use. But, if you want this in pure gold, I can get this delivered in about 7 days... you can try it – will suit your personality."

"Sure. I would like to try this stuff." saying thus she started to wear it.

"Not here – go to the wash room and then come out wearing these – you will also be able to see people's reaction – especially you husband..."

"Seems like a nice idea." she vanished toward the washroom.

Mr Kak had finished talking to the person and he looked around to see where his wife was – she couldn't be seen. Last she was seen with Riya. He walked up to her and inquired about his wife. Riya said that she had gone off to the washroom and would be back in few minutes and asked him to sit opposite her.

He took the seat even as Mrs Kak reappeared from the washroom, wearing all the accessories Riya had given her... She looked stunning.

"You look stunning." Riya and Mr Kak said almost at the same time making Mrs Kak a happier person.

"Your choice is good – what's more that you can offer to me and yes for the women in my family who I want to gift the nice accessories you got..."

Riya opened her catalogue and started showing her various items she could buy. Mr Kak in the meantime was being mesmerized by her looks and her fluent way of managing his difficult wife. At the end of all discussion, Mrs Kak had bought a variety of items and costly perfumes to the tune of 10 lakh. This was going to show off her buying skills as well make her position very strong in her family.

"Would you like cash or cheque for the payment?"

"I would prefer cash so that I can deliver these items by tomorrow and before you go to visit your family. My bank is at Rajapuri and works till 7PM. That'll give me enough time to manage everything."

"That's so sweet of you – instead of Monday, I can then travel day after tomorrow with all the gifts. So cash it will be... Darling, do we have the cash enough for this purchase or do we have to go to the bank?"

"I received a payment today morning – I have the cash in the bank which I can give you – if you could wait for few hours..."

He vanished to get the cash from is bank and Mrs Gupta who had just entered the lounge joined them. Mrs Kak introduced Riya to her and they started to discuss the products Riya had to offer. Riya was smart enough and showed her different designs and range of products which pleased Mrs Kak. She would have hated it if Mrs Gupta would have bought the same things she had bought...

When Mrs Gupta left to get her the cash, she met Mrs Srivastav, Mrs Bondre and Mrs Shaikh... They all were impressed by her glamorous looks and the rich products she had to offer and they booked their orders and gave her the cash.

All in all, the first day of her business was a great one. She had booked orders worth 35 lakh plus. She was satisfied about it and was desperate to tell this to Vicky Kundan – her husband.

She was waiting for Mrs Kak and Mrs Gupta for their cash in the lounge. They almost walked in at the same time. They gave their cash and she promised to deliver the goods to them by tomorrow afternoon which made them happy.

CHAPTER ELEVEN

She left with the cash and was trying to hire and auto when Mr Kak approached her and asked about where she was going.

"I'm going to Rajapuri to my bank where I would be depositing the cash so that I can arrange the products your wife purchased by tomorrow."

"Rajapuri ? That's hardly 2kms from here. I normally go for a walk on the riverfront park which stretches from here to Rajapuri. By road it is about 4kms – but a straight walk of only 2kms. If you want, I will accompany your walk to Rajapuri – that will save you time as well traffic jam on the way..."

She thought for a moment, "Ok – I will walk it out with you."

And they started on their walk by the riverside front park. It was a nice walkway with trees on either side and lawns spread around in between. Some points the thickness of trees almost looked like a jungle and then opened out to another lawn. The walk through the park was a refreshing one for those who loved nature.

"What's your full name?" he asked walking beside her.

"Riya – Riya Kundan. I'm wife of Vicky Kundan who maintains your cars..."

Mr Kak couldn't believe what he heard, "You mean to say that an elegant personality like you married a motor mechanic? How's this possible? You could have got someone better."

"It was arranged by my family and I couldn't say NO – so I married him. But, he is a nice man. Helpful and it's him who funded my business. I'm grateful to him."

Riya said this so to avoid any further awkward questions by Mr Kak and he was thinking how to distract her loyalty from Vicky Kundan – she was a lot more than what she deserved. She was lovely, she was elegant, she knew the ways around high class businessmen, she was beautiful and she was – sexy.

He avoided any further questions on her personal grounds but kept chatting with her and was impressed by her knowledge about business and strategies. She was brilliant. Also she showed her class when she spoke about business or for that matter any topic of high class conversation.

When they arrived at the gate of Rajapuri, she bade a bye to him leaving him totally impressed with her intelligence and her sexy charm... She obviously wanted to impress him so that she can get more business from him and his wife.

She deposited the cash at her Regional Store in Rajapuri. She picked up the products carefully packing them as per the requirements of her clients. She took her hefty commission and left the place with products and the cash.

Vicky Kundan was still working in his workshop when she arrived home. She said nothing and changed into her regular household dress. She cooked the dinner and waited for him to finish off his work and meet her for the dinner.

It was a hard day for him too. He had taken 2 more cars for maintenance. He had to pay for the loan not disturbing the cost to his house and Riya. They had their dinner without many words. She could sense that he had taken the tension to repay the loan he had taken for her.

After dinner, they lazed off – he was a bit tired of the hard work he had put on in the day.

"So – how was your day?" she asked him in anticipation that he would ask her the same and she would then tell him all about it.

"Pretty hectic..." was his tired reply, "I took on more cars so that I repay the loan I have taken. It tired me out but I can manage the instalment of the loan. How about you? How was your first day of business?"

She took a pause and left for her room. Her guess was right he was tense about repaying the loan, "Gimme a minute- I'll be right back..."

She went to her room and then on the second thoughts called him there. He entered her room with no idea what she had in her mind.

"Honey – you don't have to take any tension of repaying that loan. Especially when you have a gifted and sweet wife like me..." she looked at him and he looked at her not knowing what to say, "come – sit here and I will show you what I did on my first day of the business..."

He sat there and was totally unaware as to what she was going to say – she opened up the bags she had got from the regional HQ. She started showing him the products and reading out the cost on the labels. He was shocked with the cost of those products – he was sure they cost few more lakh rupees than the loan he had taken.

"This material is worth 35 lakh" she said with pride and "this is what I was able to sell in a single day. Not only that, I could purchase a perfume for my sweet husband who helped me stand on my feet – a perfume that costs 18000 – and this is not all..." she got up and reached her purse took out a wad of money, "to help my sweet husband and put aside his tension – this is an amount of 50K for you – the first of income from this business. You can use this to pay off first instalment of the loan you have taken on my behalf..."

He was speechless – tears rolled from his eyes. He was happy, not because his first instalment was there and that tension was over – he was happy because he had a wife who was efficient and trustworthy and he could feel she loved him...

She came closer to him and kissed him gentle and sweet. She took him in her arms and let him let out his emotions for it was him who had strived for others all his life and was not used to facing the vice-versa.

"I hope you are happy that you have a wife like me who cares" she said and kissed him again. He melted in her sweet kisses and took her in his arms and kept kissing her gently to express his love and gratitude.

"I want you to keep that money for yourself – I'll manage the loan instalment..." he said with a decision.

"No Honey, this loan is on me and I want to repay that – as soon as possible. If my business goes on like this – I will be able to do that in about 3-4 months. That will take off any tension on you and me..." she said gently, "We want a good life – don't we..."

They agreed that they will first repay the loan amount and then seek their future together.

CHAPTER TWELVE

Riya kept on meeting the prospective clients and getting more business and earned hefty commissions through them. She was thinking about how to make more money when she had a brilliant idea...

She visited Mr Kak at his office and convinced him that if he invested a small amount in her products and gifted them to his employees, they would work harder for the profits of his establishments. She, now, also had products and accessories for men.

This worked well – she began approaching offices of other clients' husbands with the same idea and it worked well for her. She was happy at the rate her business was growing.

Mrs Choksy met her to congratulate her on her big achievement in small time and had words of praise for her. While they were discussing, a couple entered and almost everyone wanted to meet them.

"Who are they?" she asked

"Mr and Mrs Anup Chand. They have returned from their foreign trip yesterday. He is the richest businessman in the town and has much money to spare. But, it's difficult to get them to buy something from here. They like and flaunt the foreign products."

"Would you like me to try and approach them?"

"Why not – they are tough nuts to crack. I have tried and failed. You can try your luck."

She observed them from far noting everything they did, their personalities and their likings – she was devising a plan to convert them into her clients.

Next day she approached Mrs Chand and impressed her with her wit and sense of fashion. Soon she bagged a big order from her and got introduced to Mr Anup Chand.

Mr Anup Chand was quite impressed by her business mind and elegance. He was happy to invite her to his office and suggest what he could do to pep up his employees.

It was all going great for Riya. She was earning hefty commissions left, right and centre. About a month form where she began, she was almost able to clear the loan Vicky Kundan had taken on her behalf.

He was astonished and happy that she was doing so well. He was not interested in the money she earned – he let her keep it and she kept stashing away in the bank where he had opened an account for her.

Mr Kak had a charming personality and she became quite friendly with him. They used to discuss his business and her business too. They were quite comfortable and she used to meet him at his office, at the lounge of the club as well his room he had booked in that club.

She was learning new techniques of selling and doing business from him and his experience as a businessman. She was expanding her business to other small townships nearby. She sometimes accompanied Mr Kak on his one day trips to these townships to gather more clients there.

Vicky Kundan on other hand had become busier. Taking the tension of the loan he had taken on more cars and was usually busy with their maintenance – early morning till late in the evenings. He hardly had time during day to spend with her. She also was busy in expanding her business.

He was working on Mr Kak's car which was almost done and had given it his finishing touch when she entered the house – quite early to his surprise.

"Hey – you early today?" he asked her casually to let her know that he was attentive. The answer to which she ran to her room and shut herself off. She had done this without saying a word.

This was quite odd. Normally, she used to be in his garage and speak about her day and business. She used to inquire about his day. Today – was different – she had gone to her room without any word.

He finished his work on Mr Kak's car and proceeded toward her room and found it locked from inside. He had to make lot of efforts before she opened the door. Her face showed that something was drastically wrong.

He sat next to her gently took her hand in his own. She pulled it away from him and started to weep. At first he couldn't understand anything as she spoke between her sobs.

He slowly coaxed her into speaking as to what had happened. She controlled her sobs and told him that Mr Kak had called her to his room for an exclusive order. When she had reached his room he put a DO NOT DISTURB sign and accosted her. She was feeling helpless but somehow managed to free herself and make an escape to their home.

His anger had no limits and he was livid because he knew Mr Kak and his womanising – he was angry because despite knowing that Riya is his wife – he had tried to take advantage of her being alone in that room. He was to deliver his car this evening and he decided to take it up –

man to man with Mr Kak.

"Don't worry – I will take care that he doesn't do it again..." he said and moved out leaving her to control her feelings. He checked for finishing touches to Mr Kak's car and drove it to the club. He got out of the car with a big spanner hidden under his sleeve and walked toward the counter.

Mr Kak wasn't there – he had gone off for his evening walk on the riverside. He dropped off the keys at the counter and made an exit. He was supposed to take an auto from there – instead he decided to walk towards Rajapuri – the thought of Mr Kak accosting Riya was playing on in his mind.

He started to walk toward Rajapuri – this was the first time he had been there – the riverside walkway and found it that it was to his advantage. It was lawns and then dense trees hiding entire walkway to from the knowledge of people who walked. He walked on wishing that he would meet Mr Kak in the density of the trees.

Sure enough, his wish came true. He was amid dense trees with nobody in sight when he came face to face with Mr Kak.

"Hey! – never seen you walk before..." Mr Kak said in surprise as he met Vicky, "how do you like here? I have been walking here since ages." Mr Kak was a bit friendly toward him which was strange.

"Ya – decided to check out this walkway." Vicky camouflaged his anger, "I have heard that this walkway is great – but I don't see the river from here – do you know where I can see the river?"

"It's a bit wayward. You have to go cross country. I will show you the view of the river amongst these dense trees – come on – this way..."

Vicky followed him on the cross country path – now they were alone amid the dense trees – nobody to watch them and what happens. They suddenly came out to the clearing and the river was is full sight. It had a strong current.

"Like it?" Mr Kak asked him.

"What's between you and Riya?" this was a straight question from Vicky.

"Oh! So you know about it – well, she is into selling her body for pleasure and charges high amount of money for that. Not only me, there are lot of wealthy people who she has been selling her body in pleasure. To tell you the truth, you are a lucky man – who can have her body without any cost and all her glamour as well her various ways of love making that makes it more pleasurable. Leave her – she is not of your kind – she is a free bird who goes where the money is flowing – just like this river."

"Liar !!!" Vicky couldn't control his anger, not only this man had accosted her but now he is proclaiming her to be a body seller. He got the spanner from his sleeve and struck Mr Kak on his head.

"Listen – I told you the truth." Mr Kak said reeling with the blow. But Vicky's anger was uncontrollable. He kept on hitting Mr Kak and when his anger subsided, he realized that Mr Kak was a dead man. He pushed his body into the river and the current made sure that it was carried away.

He washed the blood on him and slowly walked toward the path where he had been taken off by Mr Kak. He walked on the pathway not seen by anyone and reached Rajapuri. He took an auto and made his way home.

He was quiet as he was digesting the fact that he had killed a man. Finally he justified it to himself that it was the right punishment for accosting Riya – his wife and the one who depended on his protection.

After a quiet dinner, he didn't respond to her sweet kisses and just had one sentence, "Mr Kak will not trouble you again."

CHAPTER THIRTEEN

It was a week after the murder of Mr Kak. Everything was coming back to normal. He and Riya exchanged the hugs and kisses like normal. He was busy in his work and she was busy in her business. She had given him another 1 lakh against the loan he had on his head and was happy that he had only 1 more lakh to repay and was strongly working towards repayment.

"I want you to remove the speed governor in this car." Mr Gupta was insisting.

"Sir, this car is very fast and it if you drive it at even 70% of its speed capacity – would be very difficult to control. I can't do that. It's risky." Vicky was trying to explain when a police inspector walked in...

He ignored Vicky and turned to Mr Gupta, "Mr Gupta – Did Mr Kak know how to swim? Don't mind me asking this question but you have an investment in his firm and were quite close to him..."

Vicky was all ears to what transpired between the police inspector and Mr Gupta – he knew Mr Kak was killed and the killer was none other else than him...

"No – he didn't know how to swim. We had been telling him to learn swimming. Why?"

"We have found the body of Mr Kak about 50kms from here downstream the river. His body had many broken bones – I think his body must have hit the rocks and there are about 2 places where the river gushes through waterfalls. He must have slipped and fell into the river and then carried by the current onto the waterfalls and must have died because of the drowning. Doesn't it seem odd that he had disappeared for a week?"

'No – he usually used to go out on a business trips that lasted a week or more. So it was presumed that he had gone on a business trip."

"Oh! That wraps up the case. If anything is needed we will get into touch with you. By the way – any enemies of Mr Kak you know of...?"

"Nopes. It was a business relation and we were quite friendly. I don't know of any business enemy – don't know about his personal ones – he never mentioned them."

"Ok I guess this wraps up the case – have a good day Mr Gupta..." saying this, the police inspector walked off.

Vicky heaved a sigh of relief – police thought it was an accident and Mr Kak didn't know how to swim. This relaxed him thoroughly. He now turned his attention to Mr Gupta who was still in shock hearing Mr Kak's death.

"He was my partner in many ventures – it's a loss I have to check what to do with it... by the way Riya your wife had some dealings with him – did she get the payment?"

"I don't know ... I heard the news along with you."

"I can help her clear her account with Mr and Mrs Kak if there is anything pending. You have to take care that you don't go overboard with your investment till then. I can take some beating and I understand it will be difficult for you. Let me know if you need any help...and yes I would be mighty pleased if you can remove that speed governor for me..." saying thus Mr Gupta left his car and proceeded on his way.

This was a good fortune for Vicky, Mr Kak's murder was seen as an accident by the police – he was clear as far as they were concerned. They hadn't bothered to ask him any questions about the death. He wasn't considered at all ... nothing but fortunate. His problem was how will he tell this to Riya?

It was evening when she returned from her daily work and instantly was busy in cooking their meals. He waited patiently for the dinner to be eaten before he would break the news of Mr Kak's death to her.

He kept himself busy in the garage and didn't want to meet the eyes with her. Even during dinner, he kept his eyes from meeting with her eyes and was unusually quiet – no mention of what all had happened during the daily work which he normally used to relate to her.

"Riya – sit here, I want to tell you something." He said after the dinner and she sat in front of him, "Mr Kak is dead. It seems he slipped and fell into the river. Since he couldn't swim he drowned and his body has been found downstream..."

"How do you know that?"

"Today, when I was working, Mr Gupta was in the garage wanting to drop off his car, police came in and started to question him and related to this incident. Do you have any money that is stuck with him or his wife?"

"Why do you ask this? To tell you – yes, I have an outstanding with them – about 1.5 lakh. Now that he is dead I think I will have to work harder and get more clients to cover up for this loss."

"Mr Gupta said he can help you recover the amount as he was his partner in many ventures and he was going to take care of any liabilities Mr Kak had left behind... You can contact Mr Gupta, he will help you."

"Ok. I will meet him tomorrow and submit the duplicate bills. We cannot afford to take this loss to tell you the truth. But it's good riddance. Mr Kak was a bad man. The way he behaved with me serves him right. I don't feel any pity towards the news of his death..."

"Ok. Good night. That's what I had to tell you."

"Aren't you forgetting the hugs and kisses before we go to bed?"

"Oh – sorry – I was a bit disturbed by this news. His car used to be serviced by me – one customer less – means I have to search another one to recover from the loss – but how?"

"Don't worry I will be on the lookout for any such customer who has an expensive car and refer him to you..." she smiled and kissed him good night.

Next day, he started his work on Mr Gupta's car along with others. Mr Gupta like Mr Kak was a special customer and he had good relation with him. He always used to take extra efforts and care of his special customer's cars. So his work on it was a bit slow and with more care.

He knew he would have to work on that car for a week before it was ready and raring to go – so he planned his work accordingly. He worked on the other cars which were his regular but not his special customers. He wanted to make their cars ready first so that he can concentrate on his special customer's cars.

The day passed quickly in the work and he realized that Riya was waiting with the dinner. They had dinner the usual way discussing about each other's day. He was surprised that there was no mention of Mr Gupta and his word to help Riya recover the outstanding amount of Mr Kak from him...

Another day passed and still no mention of help, then another and another. He was tense because the amount was high and as Riya's husband felt he was liable to pay that amount. Though she had paid substantial amount to the loan he had taken, he still had 1 lakh to be paid and now this...

Finally he couldn't resist the temptation to ask her about the recovery of Mr Kak's amount. In reply, she promised him the amount of remaining 1 lakh saying that she will recover by doing more business with other clients and this was last instalment to his loan. He will not have to be tense about it now.

CHAPTER FOURTEEN

He let few days pass and kept wondering if Riya had contacted Mr Gupta for the recovery of money that was pending. He could bear it no longer and asked her if she had contacted Mr Gupta.

There were tears in her eyes, “I thought only a lone, beautiful woman had to face the wolves in this world ... I was wrong ... even a married woman who is beautiful has to face the wolves – especially, if her husband does small work like a motor mechanic or something similar...”

“What has happened – will you tell me with clarity?” he said gently ... knowing she was speaking the truth. He was no match for her qualification, her business sense or her beauty – and he knew that...

“I told you Mr Kak had accosted me. Mr Gupta was also along with him. They had planned to rape me one by one and quench their lust. They knew you didn’t have enough money to go to court for justice and they planned to shut off your mouth by paying heavy amount of money – if at all you create trouble...”

He felt the anger rise in him again and he wanted to kill Mr Gupta for that – but he now was aware that police will not take this as an accident and will hunt for the killer. He kept quiet and needed more time to take his revenge on Mr Gupta.

He slept thinking how he could take revenge on Mr Gupta. He kept thinking and planning and plotting – and then erasing the plans and plots as they seemed to have an error which will eventually point to him as the murderer...

One day, when he was working on one of the cars that had met with an accident, he had a brilliant idea. He called up Mr Gupta and told him that he needs a letter to remove the speed governor and it would be Mr Gupta's risk.

He was happy when the letter came to him and he carefully filed it, in case, the police asked him why he had removed the governor. Now he could easily point the blame to Mr Gupta and said that he didn't want to but couldn't deny his customer's wish...

When the car of Mr Gupta came back for removal of governor, he smiled at this and started working on it. He promised the delivery of the car next day. Mr Gupta wanted the car by evening as he was going to drive it by night, on the highway and was going to visit another town and would be glad if this was done.

He worked on the car and delivered it to Mr Gupta. Mr Gupta was absolutely pleased with the quick work and paid him some extra money. He drove off the car to the distant location on the highway – but never reached his destination. His car at very high speed collided with an oncoming truck instantly killing him. The steering wheel had locked out and the car was out of control. This was what the police found.

Next morning the news was out that he had met with an accident and was killed instantly. The news also declared that Mr Gupta was driving at a high speed and the car he was driving was totally smashed and urged people not to drive fast.

Vicky listened to the news and smiled – nobody had any doubt on him. He let Riya know that Mr Gupta had met with an accident and was killed instantly. She was happy that a tormentor was dead and put the incident on Karma.

They went with their normal routine work and she forgot everything – concentrating more on the growth of her business. She gave the half instalment of Vicky's balance loan and he was happy and a bit relieved. That eased off some pressure to work hard.

Next, she came complaining about Mr Talwar who had accosted her. Now Mr Talwar didn't drive a car – he hired them. Vicky was thinking of how he could get even with Mr Talwar – after all, he had accosted his wife... He came to know that Mr Talwar was going to address a meeting at the conference hall of Grand Club and Mr Shaikh's car was with him for repair...

He decided to visit the Grand Club at the same time with Mr Shaikh's car when Mr Talwar would be addressing the meeting and hoped he would get a chance to get even with him. He worked ferociously on Mr Shaikh's car to meet the deadline.

He reached the Grand Club and contacted Mr Shaikh who looked at the car and appreciated the work on the car. Vicky then entered the Club and sauntered near the washroom to get oil on his hands washed. He was followed by Mr Shaikh and again he appreciated the workmanship. Mr Shaikh then exited and Vicky was alone in the washroom. He hoped and prayed that Mr Talwar would visit the washroom – alone.

His prayers seemed to be answered. Mr Talwar entered the washroom alone. He knew Vicky as the mechanic who maintained all the luxury cars of the elite. He greeted him and entered the toilet enclosure. Vicky bolted the main door to the washroom after keeping the Work in Progress sign outside the door.

As soon as Mr Talwar opened the door to the toilet enclosure – he leapt on him. Mr Talwar wasn't a man of great build or strength. Soon he subdued him and strangled him to death. He closed the door to the toilet enclosure after securely putting the body of Mr Talwar in it and went the main door of the washroom, took the signboard of Work in Progress inside and went back to washing his clean hands. Two people entered the washroom and he quietly slipped out of the washroom with them...

Sometime after, near the end of the day, body of Mr Talwar was discovered and it baffled the police. So many people had visited the washroom – and nobody knew who killed him. They could see many people crossing the washroom nearby from the cameras put up outside – but couldn't find who had killed him because the washroom had no cameras installed – they were not supposed to...

Vicky was at peace but also wondered – what life had led him to – he had become a killer. He had killed at least 3 people all his customers and a person who would have become his customer the day he bought a car... He mused at what he had become and found himself alone – Riya, his wife was unperturbed and was living in her own world – slept in her bedroom and was unaware of what he had been doing for her... by the time Riya had given him all the money for the loan with interest and he had paid off to the bank.

Soon he found her complaining of other wolves accosting her and he had to kill all of them out of his anger that his wife was being accosted by them. Mr Shaikh, Mr Naidu, Mr Bhattacharya were among the people who were his customers and the balance were their associates. He didn't like the idea of killing all these people but couldn't help curbing his anger whenever Riya told him about how they had misbehaved and tried to take her advantage.

One day Riya came and showed him marks on her hand and waist which occurred due to her brawl with Mr Anup Chand who tried to force her into his bed. His rage knew no bounds. Fortunately for him, next day, Mr Chand's car had broken down on the highway and he had called him for help.

He reached the spot where Mr Anup Chand's car had broken down. His driver was trying to make it work but was unable to do that. He had checked every possibility to see where the fault lay and was not sure and had to call Vicky Kundan to the site of the breakdown.

CHAPTER FIFTEEN

Mr Anup Chand was nowhere to be seen. He went ahead and started working on the car. He had nothing to do with the driver of the car – he had not touched Riya. He found that the radiator had heated up and needed a replacement – he had new radiator in his garage.

He came back from the site for that radiator and found Riya getting ready to move out of the house for her work. She kissed him passionately as if she won't be able to kiss him again and he was left breathless. He picked up the radiator and put it in his service car and drove off. Happy that Riya loved him so much.

He reached the site and started to work on Anup Chand's car. He had almost finished the work when Anup Chand appeared from the dhaba he was resting. He was in two minds but then he restricted himself from doctoring the car – he didn't want the driver to get hurt or killed.

He finished the job on the car and took the payment. He asked the driver to fill up the radiator with water. He didn't have it in the car and the dhaba refused as they had limited stock of the water. So he asked the driver to fetch the can full of water and the driver set out on foot. The nearest village was about 2 kms and he would get to fill the water in the can there...

He was about to sit in his service car and drive off when Anup Chand asked him to wait till his driver came back with the can of water. He suggested they should sit at the dhaba and sip a cup of tea – he wanted to discuss something with Vicky Kundan...

Anup Chand let him settle down – he could see that Vicky was a bit irritated but didn't know the reason for his irritation. Vicky wanted to kill him then and there... but knew it was suicidal because there were people who would point him out and till now he had been playing it safe and knew he had to play it safe to protect Riya from such wolves...

Anup Chand looked at him and smiled before he spoke and looked away, "What is your relation with Riya?"

Vicky's anger knew no bounds yet he controlled himself for there were people around – though out of the hearing distance...

"She is my wife."

Anup Chand smirked at this reply, "Then you are not a good husband to her..."

"Why do you feel this way?"

"Well – if you were a good husband to her, she would not have to sell her body to make a living. It seems like you are a pimp who is driving her to prostitution."

"What are you saying – keep a tab on your words or else I will forget that you are one of my prestigious clients and you will face the consequence."

"Now – Now – don't get excited. I will tell you the truth. She is selling off her body for pleasure and minting money by doing so and you are the beneficiary of all that money – why can't I call you a pimp?"

'You are a liar. She works hard to earn that money and I swear I have no idea what she earns and I don't take money from her..."

"I agree that she works hard – but it's on body selling and less on her business. Believe me, she is exotic in bed. I have slept with her and the way she gives pleasure to a man is beyond description by words. If you don't push her to that – want of more money makes her do that..."

"What are you saying...?" Vicky almost choked.

"I have a feeling that you are behind the killing of all elite that have died in past few days – rightly so because you may feel that you are taking revenge or protecting her. But, what you don't know is she has been fleecing money of all those elite by offering her body at a steep charge every time they feel like enjoying her body. Why she has charged me steeply to make my esteemed clients enjoy and allow me to strike a good deal with them – even the ministers and the government officials have enjoyed her before awarding me a heavy contracts... what makes a difference if she has offered others the same services?"

Vicky was aghast at listening to Anup Chand talk like this and realized that Mr Kak had said the same things about Riya – the others had no chance of giving this information to him because he had given them no chance to speak – this created a doubt in his mind – is Riya true to him or is she like these people are talking about? He remained silent knowing that Anup Chand's allegation that he was involved in killing of all those elite was correct and he could blow a whistle on him to the police. He had to play this one patiently.

"I don't know what you are talking about..." was his short reply to Anup Chand.

"Ok – man to man – here's the deal. You divorce Riya and let me take care of her – I can make more money by leasing out her body – she wants money not you which I will pay her in abundance. I will pay you one million for this deal and I have that sum ready here – right now...” he pushed a packet in Vicky’s hand, “anyways, she has been unfaithful to you – why bother? And another promise for doing so – I will keep your hand in all these killings a secret – you will go scot free...agreed?”

Vicky was not interested in money – but the root of suspicion had taken shape in his mind about Riya and her misadventures – he wanted to find if that was true...

“Ok – deal. One thing, if what you said about Riya is false – I will stick this entire bundle down your throat and choke your breath till you die...”

Anup Chand laughed at this – “You won’t have to choke me. Now here’s my other car, I will take this one till I know that you have not doctored the broken one. I will wait for your answer...”

He sat in the other car and drove off. His driver came back with water and filled up the radiator and started the car. They both drove toward their town. Anup Chand’s car reached without any mishap and Vicky proceeded to his home. He had to find the truth ...

CHAPTER SIXTEEN

Vicky was in two minds – should he confront Riya on this – or should he be a good husband and trust her ... yet he had two people saying she did betray him and they were not connected. Further, one of them was killed the first by him and the other one was alive. He looked at the packet of 1 million and threw it in disgust on his bed and decided for Riya to show up...

He was surprised to find another packet on his bed – it contained another million rupees. He was at a loss to understand how come there are 2 packets containing one million each when Anup Chand had given only one packet. Riya normally showed up a lunch time and they had their lunch together – if she was delayed or had an appointment – she used to inform this earlier. Today was different, Riya had not informed him of the delay or the appointment – she was late for lunch...

Feeling hungry, he looked up in the kitchen. There was no food kept for him neither had the earlier day's utensils been washed. All kinds of negative thoughts started to gather in his mind – was Riya in any sort of trouble? Was Riya alright? She was at home when he had left to meet Anup Chand – did someone come and abduct her – you never know rich people could do anything...

He decided to wait for her to return for some time before hitting the panic button. It was a long and panicky wait. He thought that she would be busy and to help her out – he went out and bought lunch packs which they could eat. Still no sign of Riya...

Finally, he called her up. The phone kept ringing with no answer. Again all kinds of negative thoughts about Riya's safety gripped him. He called her again and it kept on ringing without any answer... Feeling hungry, he ate the lunch he had bought and then called up again to a ringing tone – no answer. He didn't know what to do or where to look for her...

Suddenly his phone rang – it was Riya, "What's the matter with you – why are you calling me?" she sounded irritated.

"Where are you? Are you safe? – I had a meeting with Anup Chand and wanted to discuss few matters with you..."

"Oh! Forget him ... he means nothing to me. I don't want to discuss him or any of his talks."

He could faintly hear the beat of railway train in the background as if she was travelling in it – he was confused.

"Where are you?"

"Oh! I am in a train – going far away from that dirty town of yours."

"You are going without telling me or informing me – your husband?"

"Wake up! You are not my husband. The whole story of us getting married in front of that temple was a farce and a way to make you happy and allow me to stay at your home. I never married you. We are strangers and will remain so in future. Don't show any tantrums that you are my husband. I have kept one million for you on your bed for letting me stay with you and earn my money."

"What do you mean?" he wondered. He felt his heart sinking.

"Are you so dumb? Listen – I used you and your business to get in touch with all the rich elites in your town. Then I approached them and impressed them with my looks and glamour. They were wolves alright – they fell for it. They first started giving me business which was fair enough earning – if I were really your wife. But my aim was to fleece them of all their money."

"Go on ..." he said now anger sweeping across him.

"I played it tough for them to make them desperate enough to splash money on me. I also told them a sorry state that I was in because I was married to you and how badly you treated me – I lied that you had an affair with your neighbour's wife and I was all alone in this big bad world – just like I had told you when we first met..."

"So I was the bad guy..."

"Sorry darling, you were a thorough gentleman and didn't even touch me and kept your word. But this story was for them and they fell for it. Then slowly I allowed them to touch me and kiss me showing their concern – the false concern for me. I knew what they wanted and I was absolutely slow in letting them sleep with me. In return they gave me money with advice that I leave you and they would take care of me. This way I would be free and all available to them to play with my body which they were doing even when they suggested me."

He was listening with intent for any other sound that will give away her location.

"It was good while it lasted... They paid for me through their nose and I was happy collecting money and showing them that I loved them true. You won't believe I have earned in crores. I had done something similar in last town where I met you. Then these so called elites started using my body to impress their clients. I had to sleep with them to get them massive orders and strike fabulous deals. They started paying me all the more heavily."

"Go on ..." he said now the anger hitting the highest point.

"Soon Kak ran out of his money and still wanted all the pleasures that he had derived when he was paying me. That's when I told you that he had accosted me. I thought you would threaten the life out of him – but you took life out of him and killed him. You think I wouldn't guess this – you were wrong. You have killed all those men who I had complained about that they had accosted me. I didn't think you would be so good at playing this dangerous game of murder. Nobody had any doubts on you – even police who are so efficient in solving murders didn't doubt you. So far so good – but you never know they might be on your trail any moment. So being a sweet wife I left one million for you to take and make a dash for it before the police rounded you up and charged with murder..."

"Where are you going?"

"That's another town with another name. I found it easier to get suckers with a story like you and me getting married. I liked this modus operandi. So I met this timid guy whose name is Umesh Shah – I similarly made him think I am married to him and now I am going to his town with a new name. I won't be Rekha Meerut or Riya Kundan – I will be known as Jalpa Shah... Mrs Jalpa Shah. If you are able to make a run before police get you, find me and I will give you another list of people to kill. You kill them and earn your next million – how interesting and romantic – Wow!"

He couldn't believe what he had heard – can a beautiful girl like her can be so sadistic?

"Any ways – the train is approaching a bridge on a river and I am going to throw this phone in there. Nobody from my past will be able to approach me or nab me. Thank you for all you did for me and take my advice – run for your life and this is the last conversation you have with me – unless you find me again and this time I promise you pleasure my body if you do – till then my last kiss Sssssmmmmmoooooccccchhhhh..."

The phone got disconnected even as he heard the train passing over a bridge. He tried calling again but the phone was out of coverage area. He was livid at being used that turned him into a murderer. They all were men – innocent, trapped by this gorgon. He thought and checked the train time table for all the trains that departed from the station that day. He found two trains leaving at noon in two directions and similarly there were two trains leaving in the evening in the same two directions.

He called up his assistant and others who worked with him. He told them that his mother was sick and perhaps on deathbed and he will have to go to attend her. He gave the keys to his garage to them asking them to take care of it and earn money till he returned. They were concerned about his mother and happy that they would be able to earn more money till he returned.

He packed a small bag pack, kept in the 2 million in there which he would use to find Riya – she didn't deserve to live. She would destroy many men that she would meet in her crazy endeavour to make money in her life. She deserved death. He already knew that he would be tried for all the murders he had committed – what difference will it make if he has to kill Riya as well...

His only dilemma was which direction had Riya travelled. He went to the station and thought about it. After a hard thinking process, he bought a ticket going in one direction thinking that if it was a wrong one he would take a train reverse direction. But the search for her was on...

He would eventually find Riya and kill her...

Acknowledgements

Thank You for Reading this story and we do hope that this did entertain you.

We at 'BakBak' (YouTube Channel) are glad to be associated with Prasad Deshpande and we take pride in promoting his amazingly different concept stories... This channel is for the dialogs and scenes that were edited and couldn't make it to the print. Because his stories are in English and these are either in other languages or not in line with stories.

His other published books are as given below...

The Conducer

(A political mystery thriller)

My Fiancée's Boyfriend

(Romantic thriller – Not a Love Triangle)

Red Clipper

(An entertaining story of a RAW soldier who saves millions of lives)

To get to his stories just type "prasad deshpande" on Amazon.com

We are planning to launch his best of the stories in coming months...

Wait for it...

We request you to send your feedback on the email ...

pdsspartners @ gmail.com

Or, Follow the Author Pages managed by us and his close friends...

Instagram - @ pen2me

Facebook/thiscanhappentoyou

(Seen as "Flights of Fantasy")

For his other very short and other free works you can follow his account on Facebook ...

Facebook/pen2me

.... a "BakBak" promotion.

9 798890 025937

Printed by Libri Plureos GmbH in Hamburg,
Germany